# The Dead Sea Squirrels Series

## Merle of Nazareth

# Mike Nawrocki

Illustrated by Luke Séguin-Magee

Tyndale House Publishers
Carol Stream, Illinois

Visit Tyndale's website for kids at tyndale.com/kids.

Visit the author's website at mikenawrocki.com.

*TYNDALE* is a registered trademark of Tyndale House Ministries. The Tyndale Kids logo is a trademark of Tyndale House Ministries.

*The Dead Sea Squirrels* is a registered trademark of Michael L. Nawrocki.

*Merle of Nazareth*

Designed by Libby Dykstra

Edited by Sarah Rubio

Published in association with the literary agency of Brentwood Studios, 1550 McEwen, Suite 300 PNB 17, Franklin, TN 37067.

*Merle of Nazareth* is a work of fiction. Where real people, events, establishments, organizations, or locales appear, they are used fictitiously. All other elements of the novel are drawn from the author's imagination.

For manufacturing information regarding this product, please call 1-855-277-9400.

For information about special discounts for bulk purchases, please contact Tyndale House Publishers at csresponse@tyndale.com, or call 1-855-277-9400.

**Library of Congress Cataloging-in-Publication Data**

A catalog record for this book is available from the Library of Congress.

ISBN 978-1-4964-4973-3

Printed in the United States of America

27   26   25   24   23   22   21
8    7    6    5    4    3    2

*With gratitude and thanks*
*for Michael and Justin's real-life teachers*
*at Walnut Grove Elementary, Pearre Creek*
*Elementary, and Battle Ground Academy.*

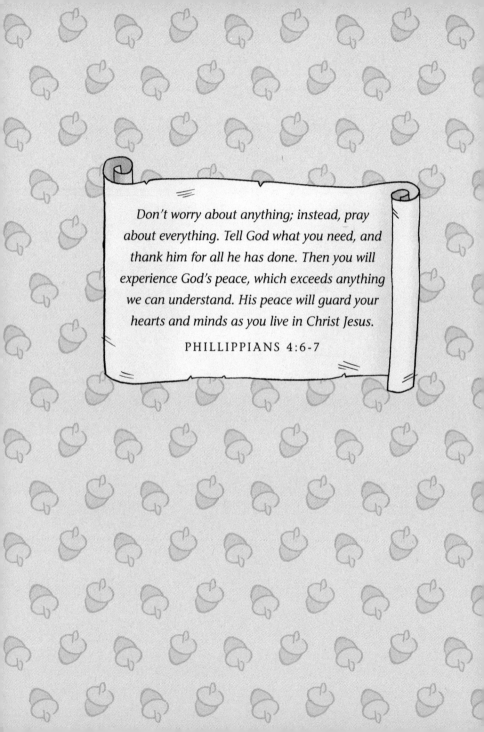

*Don't worry about anything; instead, pray about everything. Tell God what you need, and thank him for all he has done. Then you will experience God's peace, which exceeds anything we can understand. His peace will guard your hearts and minds as you live in Christ Jesus.*

PHILLIPPIANS 4:6-7

# BUT WAIT!

## BEFORE WE START...

## Who are the Dead Sea Squirrels?

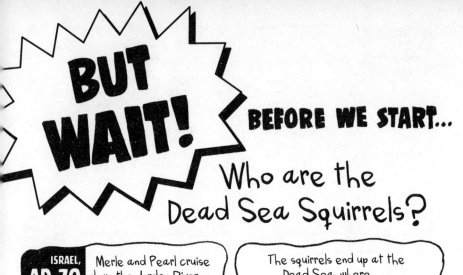

**ISRAEL, AD 70** Merle and Pearl cruise down the Jordan River...

...on the vacation of a lifetime!

The squirrels end up at the Dead Sea, where...

You can't sink! I've always wanted to not sink!

Couldn't you have just worn your floaties in the lake back home?

Soon the two salty squirrels are hot, thirsty, and desperate for shade. Then they spot a cave.

Merle's sense of adventure lures him into the cave, despite Pearl's protests.

If God wanted you to go into a cave, he would have made you a bat.

Ten-year-old Michael Gomez is spending the summer at the Dead Sea with his professor dad and his best friend, Justin.

While exploring a cave (without his dad's permission), Michael discovers two dried-out, salt-covered critters and stashes them in his backpack.

Michael sneaks the squirrels back home with him to Tennessee.

He sets them up like posable action figures on his dresser—under an open window.

While Michael is sleeping, a thunderstorm rolls in, and it begins to rain...

...rehydrating the squirrels!

Up and kicking again after almost 2,000 years, Merle and Pearl Squirrel have great stories and advice to share with the modern world.

# They are the Dead Sea Squirrels!

But the Dead Sea Squirrels' adventures don't end there. Merle and Pearl soon find out that things are

## a whole lot different

from the first century!

For one thing, there are self-filling fresh water bowls . . .

an endless supply of walnuts and chicken nuggets . . .

Thank you, chickens, for your nuggets!

and much fancier places to live!

I could get used to this!

Plus, they get to go to fifth grade (as long as no one sees them)!

Stay still, Merle! Pretend you are stuffed!

# CHAPTER 1

# DING!

"The captain has turned off the fasten seat belt sign," a woman's voice announced over the flight loudspeaker.

"Yes!" Merle whispered to Pearl, who was snuggled into the window seat with him. "This belt is so constricting." He unclicked the seat belt that had been stretched over both squirrels and stretched out his legs with a sigh.

"Please keep your seat belts fastened at all times when seated," the woman's voice continued.

"Oh, for Pete's sake," Merle complained. "Which is it? Off or on?!"

"SHHHHH! I told you to not speak," hushed the man in the suit and sunglasses. Merle and Pearl now knew their squirrelnapper by his actual name: Ruben. The evening before, the squirrels had been tricked by his ingenious drone scheme, and they had all but airmailed themselves right into his clutches. In the hours that followed, they were whisked to the airport, fitted into oversize emotional support dog vests (which, even though they were designed for Chihuahuas, were way too roomy for squirrels), and loaded onto an international flight.

"Sir, did you say you'd like the steak?" a flight attendant asked as she rolled up with the food cart.

Merle nodded his head vigorously.

"Oh, look at you!" the flight attendant gushed at him. "Aren't you adorable?" She turned to Ruben. "It's like your little support squirrel knows what I'm saying. He probably wants another bag of nuts!" She giggled.

Merle shook his head with equal vigor and held out his paws for a steak, earning an elbow to the side from Pearl and a look of disbelief from the flight attendant.

"Thank you, miss." Ruben grabbed the steak tin and set it on his seat table.

3

"Could I also get another one for my little friends? They are such a support to me."

"I'm sure they are . . ." the flight attendant said, still looking shocked. She handed Ruben another steak meal. "Be sure they stay buckled while seated." She gave them an uncomfortable smile and slunk away.

"When you get a chance, can you ask her for a cheese tray? Gorgonzola would be tremendous with this steak," Merle whispered to Ruben, holding up the business class flight menu.

"SHHHHH!" Ruben shushed grumpily as Pearl buckled herself and Merle up again.

# CHAPTER 2

A large map of Israel lay spread out across the Gomezes' kitchen table. The entire family, along with Michael's best friends, Justin and Sadie, stared at two acorns and a tiny little Monopoly iron that rested on the map. You might have thought the group was playing a board game. But this was no game! Dr. Gomez and Michael were planning a rescue mission.

"The acorns are the squirrels?" Jane, Michael's little sister asked, holding the family cat, Mr. Nemesis, on her lap.

"Yes," Michael said impatiently. With that confirmation, Mr. Nemesis reached a paw out and thwacked the acorns, sending them flying. "Bad cat!" Michael hollered.

"Why is there an iron?" Jane wondered.

"The iron represents the man in the suit and sunglasses. It was the only other game piece I could find," Michael said, picking the acorns up from the floor.

⭐ dss popular  •••

♡ liked by no one

⭐ dss popular  •••

liked by sadie_ssquid
and thousands of others

Justin nodded. "Nobody ever wants to be the iron."

"Yeah, what's with the iron?" Sadie added. "I'm always the hat."

"I like the race car," said Justin.

"C'mon guys, we need to concentrate!" Michael barked. "Dad, where do you think he's taking them?"

"They will most likely fly into Tel Aviv," Dr. Gomez said. "It's one of Israel's three international airports and the biggest. It's where we flew in and out of this summer." Dr. Gomez moved the acorns and the iron on the map, over the Mediterranean Sea to Tel Aviv. "From there, my best guess is that they will head straight to Jerusalem by car—about an hour's drive." He scooted the trio of tiny objects over to Jerusalem.

"Or less if you use the race car," Justin whispered to Sadie, earning a glare from Michael.

"Not back to the Dead Sea?" Mrs. Gomez wondered.

"I don't think so," Dr. Gomez said. "The man in the suit and sunglasses is working for a collector. Merle and Pearl wouldn't be of much value to a collector at the Dead Sea."

"Well, that's good, at least," Mrs. Gomez said. Merle and Pearl had said more than once that they had no desire to return to the Dead Sea area. It was way too dry and salty for squirrels there.

"If we can find out who the collector is, we can most likely find Merle and Pearl." Dr. Gomez frowned at the map.

"But what if we can't find them, Dad?" Michael said. "I'm scared I'll never get to see Merle and Pearl again." He sighed. "I wish we had some kind of a clue where they're headed."

# CHAPTER 3

"If only we had some sort of clue where we're headed . . ." Pearl whispered in squirrel to Merle as Ruben sat next to them, his seat pushed back, reading. "Michael's probably worried about us."

"I'm worried about us, too!" Merle replied, also in squirrel. "What do you think Ruben's plan is?"

"I don't know, and I don't want to find out." Pearl sighed and looked around the plane. "Wait. Hold on a second . . ."

Merle turned to see what had caught her attention. Two teenage girls sat across the aisle from them, snapping selfies with their smartphones.

"It's so lame that we don't get free Wi-Fi," one girl said, patting her hair.

"We can post when we land," her friend responded. She made duck lips at her camera. "Kati's gonna be super jealous we're flying first class."

"Business class."

"Whatever. Same difference."

Pearl's eyes lit up. "Merle! I have an idea!" She poked her husband in the side. "You need to go to the bathroom."

"Um, no, I don't," Merle said.

"Yes, you do!" Pearl insisted. "Tell Ruben you need to go. I need a moment with those girls."

Needless to say, Ruben was not happy to have his reading interrupted by Merle's request. "Can't you just hold it?"

"At his age?" Pearl quipped.

Not wanting to take his eyes off either squirrel, Ruben attempted to take them both to the bathroom. Fortunately for Pearl and her plan, he was stopped by the flight attendant. "One at a time, sir." She handed Ruben a puppy pee pad. Which, in case you've ever

13

wondered, is how pottying works for pets on a plane.

"No funny moves from you, got it?" Ruben warned Pearl, who smiled innocently and headed back to her seat.

Actually, funny moves were exactly what Pearl had in mind. No sooner had the sliding door of the airplane lavatory closed than Pearl hopped up on her seatback table and began to bust a move.

"Becky! Look at that!" One of the girls across the aisle giggled. "Check out that weird little dancing dog."

Pearl twisted, vogued, and dougied, dancing silently at 30,000 feet. She had always enjoyed dancing, and had  recently picked up some new moves online while Michael was at school.

"That's not a dog. It's some kind of fluffy ferret," Becky laughed as the girls pointed their phones at Pearl and began recording.

# CHAPTER 4

The Gomez family minivan zoomed down the interstate toward the airport. Michael's and Dr. Gomez's backpacks, stuffed full for a trip of unknown length, were crammed between the lift-gate and the back seat where Michael, Justin, and Sadie sat.

"I was hoping I would get to come with you on your next trip," lamented Sadie. Michael had brought only Justin with him on his dad's Dead Sea dig the previous summer, where they had found Merle and Pearl. Michael had promised Sadie she could come the next time.

"Who knew that our next trip would

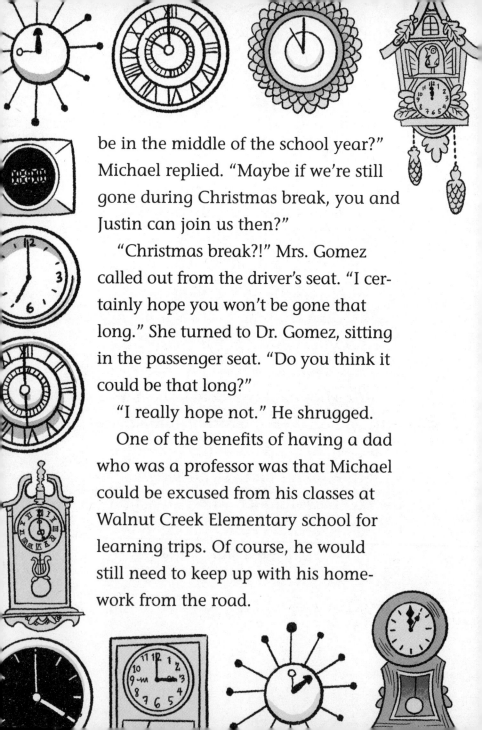

be in the middle of the school year?" Michael replied. "Maybe if we're still gone during Christmas break, you and Justin can join us then?"

"Christmas break?!" Mrs. Gomez called out from the driver's seat. "I certainly hope you won't be gone that long." She turned to Dr. Gomez, sitting in the passenger seat. "Do you think it could be that long?"

"I really hope not." He shrugged.

One of the benefits of having a dad who was a professor was that Michael could be excused from his classes at Walnut Creek Elementary school for learning trips. Of course, he would still need to keep up with his homework from the road.

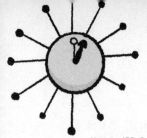

"We'll help however we can from here," Justin said.

"Yeah! We can track you online and do research," Sadie added. "There's an eight-hour time difference, but we can video chat before school in the morning—which will be your afternoon. It'll take some getting used to."

If you've ever wondered how it's possible that at the exact moment you are going to bed at night, another kid on the other side of the planet is just waking up in the morning, it's because the world is round. The earth takes 24 hours to spin around once—that means there are also 24 time zones. Israel happens to be 8 times zones ahead of Tennessee, so when Justin

and Sadie were waking up at 7 a.m. in Tennessee, it would be the middle of the afternoon (3 p.m.) in Israel for Michael. And when Michael woke up at 7 a.m. in Israel, it would be 11 p.m. the night before in Tennessee. It can be confusing at first, and one thing's for sure— at some point, somebody's gonna accidentally wake someone else up.

Mrs. Gomez pulled the minivan to the curb in the departures lane, and Michael and Dr. Gomez climbed out. Justin and Sadie helped with the backpacks as Jane remained buckled into her car seat.

"We'll be praying for you," Mrs. Gomez said, hugging her son. "And if you're feeling scared or worried about Merle and Pearl, you can also pray and ask God for help."

"Thanks, Mom. I will," Michael said as Justin helped him put on his back-pack. After a few more hugs and high fives, Dr. Gomez and Michael headed into the terminal.

# CHAPTER 5

In another airport, nearly half a
world away, Merle and Pearl glided
through the terminal in a rolling pet
carrier. "This is so humiliating," Merle
complained as passing travelers
peeked in at them through
the mesh with puzzled
expressions.

23

"As bad as George Washingsquirrel?" Pearl smiled, recalling the time Michael had brought the squirrels to school dressed in outfits borrowed from George and Martha Washington dolls.

"No. Not as bad as that. But at least those clothes fit." Merle called up to Ruben, "You mind telling us where you're taking us?"

"As a matter of fact, I do mind. But you will find out soon enough," Ruben

replied, pulling them onto an escalator.
As they descended toward the baggage
claim, the squirrels spotted a sign reading "Welcome to Haifa" in both English
and Hebrew.

"Haifa? Where's Haifa?" Merle whispered to Pearl.

"I have no idea," she answered. In
fact, in Merle and Pearl's day, early in
the first century, a city called Haifa did
not yet exist. It was given that name
much later.

"I hope it's not near the Dead Sea,"
Merle said. "If I'm afraid of anything,
it's going back there."

"You and me both." Pearl shud-
dered as they rolled up to the rental
car counter.

"Maybe one of those will tell us
where we are." Merle pointed to a rack

of maps sitting next to them. As Ruben spoke with the rental car agent, Merle tried to unzip the carrier enough to reach out a paw and grab a map. With the squirrels on the inside and the zipper handle on the outside, however, it was no use. "I can't get it open," Merle groaned.

Just then, a little girl approached the counter with her mother. She was just a little bit taller than Merle and Pearl's luggage prison, but close enough to hear a whisper.

"Pssst!" Merle called out quietly.

"Down here." The girl looked down at the squirrels and giggled. "Could you please hand me one of those maps?" Merle pointed to the map rack. The girl's gaze followed. With her free hand she obediently grabbed a map and held it out for the squirrels. Merle pointed to the luggage zipper. Understanding perfectly, the girl let go of her mom's hand, unzipped the luggage, and slipped Merle the map before her mother could react.

"What are you doing?" the girl's mom demanded.

"Talking to the silly squirrels," the girl responded.

"Sweetie, you can't touch people's luggage. I am so sorry," the mom apologized to Ruben.

"Grmph," Ruben grunted grumpily at the mom and the girl as he reached down and re-zipped the luggage. Thankfully, he didn't notice the map. As they rolled away toward their rental car, Merle and Pearl gave the helpful little girl a thankful wave.

# CHAPTER 6

Merle and Pearl wasted no time in unfolding the map once Ruben threw their canvas prison into the back seat of the rental car. Merle scanned the map and quickly found their location at Haifa Airport. "Look, Pearl—we're up north by Mount Carmel!" Way before even Merle and Pearl's time, Mount Carmel was made famous when the prophet Elijah went there and called down fire from heaven.

"Wait," Pearl said. "We're near Galilee!"

Merle caught a glimpse of a road sign out the window. "And we're headed east—toward Nazareth!" he whispered. This was great news for Merle—that's where he'd grown up! It was a small town that he knew like the back of his paw.

"Remember the first time we met?" Pearl asked, pointing to a spot on the map along the Sea of Galilee.

"I was just a small-town squirrel on my first trip to the big city," Merle recalled. Pearl was from Tiberias, along the shore of Galilee. "You seemed so sophisticated."

"And I still am!" Pearl smiled.

"Here's where we started our raft ride." Merle pointed to the southern end of the sea, which fed into the Jordan River. Merle's bright idea to sail down the Jordan for a vacation at the Dead Sea was the reason the squirrels ended up petrified in a cave for 2,000 years.

"Don't remind me," Pearl said dryly.

Merle turned his attention back to the matter at hand. "If we manage to escape once we get to Nazareth, at least we'll be in familiar territory," he said.

"That's a big if," Pearl replied, keeping an eye on their squirrel-napper.

# CHAPTER 7

BLOOOING
BLOOOING
ZPHLTTT!

The sounds of *Super Squish Squids 3* rang out from Sadie's video game console. *Super Squish Squids* was her absolute favorite video game, made even more fun for her due to the fact that it was also Michael's favorite. The two shared a friendly rivalry in which Sadie always seemed to remain a couple of levels ahead.

Sadie let out a sigh as she conquered

level 12. Now that Michael was out of the country for who-knew-how long, the game didn't feel quite as fun.

"Sadie, time for bed!" her mom's voice called from the study.

Much to her mom's surprise, rather than bargaining for a few more minutes of playing time, which is what pretty much every kid does when told to turn off their video game, Sadie replied, "Yes, ma'am," and turned off the game.

"Is everything okay?" Her mom peeked around the corner into the family room, raising an eyebrow.

"Yeah . . ." Sadie sighed again. "I think I'll wait until Michael gets back before I start on the next level."

Her mom smiled warmly before popping back into the study. "I'll be in to tuck you in and pray in a minute."

Just then, a text alert chimed on Sadie's phone. She looked down to find a text from her friend Maddie: **Adorable.** Maddie was a big fan of cute animal memes, so Sadie clicked on the link, fully expecting to find an adorable animal.

A video popped up. "Dancing ferret on flight to Haifa!" the caption read. Sadie squinted at the looped footage of a small, furry animal doing the Dougie on an airplane seatback table. A small, furry animal wearing a tiny string of pearls.

"What?!" Sadie shouted out loud.

"I said I'll be in to tuck you in and pray in a minute," her mom repeated.

Sadie immediately texted Maddie.

**Where did you get this?!**

going around.
OBVS not a ferret.
still ♥ ♥ ♥.

Sadie ran to the study. "Mom! Can I use your computer?"

"I thought you were going to bed?" her mom said, turning around from her keyboard.

"Just for two seconds, please!"

"I knew it was too good to be true." Mrs. Henderson smiled as she offered Sadie the chair.

Sadie googled Haifa. "Haifa—
the third largest city in Israel—after
Jerusalem and Tel Aviv," she read. "Oh
my goodness, they flew in to a different
airport!"

"Who did?" her mom asked.

"Michael and his dad!" Sadie picked
up her phone to forward Michael the
link from Maddie. **M & P flew into a different airport!** she added before hitting
send.

# CHAPTER 8

In a perfect world either every airline would offer free texting on all international flights, OR every ten-year-old boy would have an extra $20 to blow on Wi-Fi. But that's not the world we live in, so Sadie's urgent and important message would have to wait. Instead, high above the Atlantic Ocean, a very groggy Michael continued fighting off going to sleep.

"What are we going to do once we land in Tel Aviv?" he asked his dad with a yawn.

"I think our best bet is to head straight for Jerusalem," Dr. Gomez answered, also with a yawn. "We'll

HAIFA

MEDITERRANEAN SEA

ISRAEL

TEL AVIV

SEA OF GAL...

grab a car—it'll be less than an hour's drive." He opened up a map on the seatback table and pointed out the route.

"Why didn't we just fly into Jerusalem?" Michael wondered.

"Good question." Dr. Gomez noted, "It's Israel's biggest city, but doesn't have an airport. It's not that big of a deal, though, because the country isn't that big. With Haifa Airport in the north and Tel Aviv in the south, you can reach most places fairly quickly by car." Michael looked at the map as Dr. Gomez pointed out the locations of the cities. "Once we get to Jerusalem, we can visit my contact at the Antiquities Museum."

O JERUSALEM

N
W    E
S

DEAD SEA

Michael nodded, then turned to gaze out the window over the moonlit Atlantic Ocean.

"I know you're worried, but you should try to get some sleep," his dad said quietly. "You ready for bedtime prayers?"

"Sure." Michael nestled into his miniature flight pillow and paper-thin blanket.

"Dear God," Dr. Gomez prayed softly, "you tell us that instead of worrying, we should pray. Thank you for all you have done to keep us safe. We ask that you keep Merle and Pearl safe tonight and help us to find them. Please give us your peace and guard our hearts and minds as we sleep."

41

Before his dad could get to, "In Jesus' name, amen," Michael was out cold.

# CHAPTER 9

"Where in the world are we?!" Merle
gasped from behind the black mesh of
the rolling pet carrier in the back seat
of the rental car.

In the seat directly in front of them,
Ruben inched slowly through afternoon traffic.

"This isn't what I remember," Merle
said.

In fact, the modern city of Nazareth,
with a human population of close to
70,000 people, bore almost no resem-
blance to the town of 400 Merle had
grown up in. Although most likely the
squirrel population remained about
the same.

As Merle marveled at the changes in the town of his youth, Pearl had managed to figure out an escape plan. If you've ever tried to keep squirrels from raiding a bird feeder, this won't come as a surprise. Squirrels are really good at solving problems, and Pearl was better than most. In his haste to get Merle and Pearl away from the little girl in the airport, Ruben had failed to zip the pet carrier completely closed. Pearl noticed some daylight peeking through and was able to squeeze one of her front paw toes into the gap between

44

the top stop and the slider of the
zipper. "Merle! Give me a push,"
she whispered. "I've almost got it."

"Got what?" Merle asked, distracted.

"Our way out. Remember?"

"Oh yeah! Sorry. Just reminiscing."
Merle grabbed Pearl around the waist
and pushed her forward. Pearl's toe
also pushed forward, slowly unzipping the carrier until she created
a gap large enough to slip through.
Thankfully, the sounds of the city
outside Ruben's open driver's-side
window were loud enough to mask
the sound of unzipping.

Merle and Pearl, still dressed
in their emotional support vests,
crawled slowly out of the carrier,
keeping an eye on
Ruben. The car

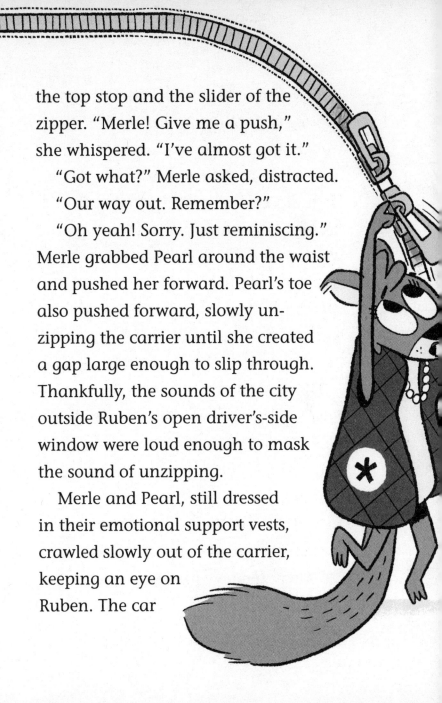

had picked up a little speed, but Merle spotted a stoplight up ahead. If they were going to escape, they needed to do it when the car was not moving. He nudged Pearl and pointed at the light. He then pointed to the automatic window opener on the rear passenger-side door. Merle had taken enough car rides with Michael to know how those worked. Pearl nodded, understanding the plan.

The car rolled up to the red light, slowing down. Merle and Pearl tensed, ready to spring into action.

Just then, Ruben turned to check on the squirrels.

"AHHHHH!" Two squirrels and one human screamed at once, shocked to see each other eye to eye.

Merle recovered first and dove for

the electric window opener.
"Jump!" he shouted, pressing
the button.

Pearl squeezed through
the opening window. Ruben
reached to try and grab Merle
as Pearl leaped from the window onto the sidewalk. "Get
out, Merle!" she shouted.

Merle made a mighty leap
for the open window, avoid-
ing Ruben's swatting hand.
As Merle sailed through the
opening, freedom milliseconds
away, his emotional support
vest snagged on the knob of
the door lock. He snapped back
and smacked the outside of the
car door, hanging helplessly
from his vest by his armpits.

Ruben's hand reached out to grab
Merle!

"Merle!" Pearl shouted.

"I'm really not a fan of this vest!"
Merle yelled, trying desperately to
wiggle free.

Ruben stretched farther into the
back seat to snag the escaping squirrel.
However, Ruben had not brought the
car to a complete stop. With his attention on Merle, he didn't notice a car in
front of him. *CRUNCH!* The impact of
the two cars colliding sent Merle sail-
ing forward, screaming, out of his vest
and head-over-tail into a street-side
potted plant!

# CHAPTER 10

A very groggy Michael and Dr. Gomez exited the plane in Tel Aviv Airport. One of the results of jetting across so many time zones is something called "jet lag." It usually takes a day or so for your body to get used to the shift in time. Blinking sleepily, Michael paused to turn on his phone and try to find a Wi-Fi signal.

"Hey buddy, let's keep moving—you can check your messages later," Dr. Gomez said, urging Michael forward.

"Yes, sir." Michael stuck his phone back in his pocket. Sadie's important tip would have to wait! However, now that he was in Israel, Michael could

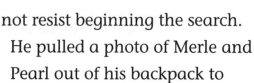

not resist beginning the search. He pulled a photo of Merle and Pearl out of his backpack to show to passing airport workers. "Have you seen these squirrels?" he asked the gate agent.

She beamed at him. "No. But I have seen an adorable little boy."

Michael cringed with embarrassment, smiled impatiently, then moved to catch up to his dad. He spotted a familiar-looking security guard. "Where have I seen him before?" he thought to himself as he showed the picture to the guard.

"Nope. Never seen 'em," the guard replied, scowling.

Michael then remembered that this was the same guard who had missed seeing the petrified Merle and Pearl as they passed through the X-ray machine when Michael left the country at the end of the summer. "No. Of course you haven't. Thank you." He hurried on.

After he and his dad showed the immigration agent their passports, Michael showed her the picture. She shook her head.

As they headed out of the terminal toward their rental car, Michael passed by a teenage girl looking at her phone, giggling at the latest internet meme. "Dancing squirrel—hilarious!" she chirped—just after the sliding doors closed behind Michael.

# CHAPTER 11

"Merle! Merle!" Pearl shouted into the geraniums. "Are you okay?!"

Merle popped his head out of the leaves. "Now that I'm out of that vest, I'm fine," he said.

Pearl looked down at her vest. "Mine's kind of growing on me . . . it goes nicely with my pearls, don't you think?"

Merle looked down the street and stiffened. "I think we need to run!" Ruben was headed toward them on foot. He, in turn, was being chased by the disgruntled motorist he'd rear-ended.

After a few blocks of running,

climbing, and jumping, the squirrels felt pretty sure they had lost Ruben. "Where to now?" Merle wondered, catching his breath.

"You tell me!" Pearl replied. "This is your town."

"It's completely different! I have no idea where we are!" Merle said. "And we left the map in the car."

"Shalom!" a voice squeaked out in squirrel from a nearby tree. Merle and Pearl turned and looked up to see an elderly Persian squirrel, also known

as the Caucasian squirrel, the same
species as Merle and Pearl. *Shalom* is
a greeting in Hebrew (and squirrel)
that means "peace." "You look lost.
Tourists?"

"Shalom, brother!" Merle replied.
"It's been a while since I've been here.
I'm a little turned around. Maybe you
could point us toward the synagogue?"
In the first century, most villages in
Israel had a synagogue, a Jewish place
of worship, in the heart of the town.
Merle figured he might be able to get
his bearings if he found a familiar
landmark.

"Which one? There are tons of

them," the friendly squirrel replied. "Plus, you're in the wrong part of town for that. This is the Latin quarter— you're more likely to find a church here. There's actually a really famous one a few blocks up. You can't miss it." The squirrel pointed down the street.

Not having any better ideas, Merle and Pearl thanked the helpful local and the three squirrels all said "Shalom!" again to each other. Then Merle and Pearl headed in the recommended direction. Sure enough, three blocks down, they came upon a large, beautiful church.

"Basilica of the Annunciation," Pearl read on a plaque near the door.

Merle shrugged. "Let's check it out." The two squirrels scurried up the wall and into an open window.

# CHAPTER 12

"Welcome back to Jerusalem!" Dr. Simon beamed as Dr. Gomez and Michael entered his office at the Antiquities Museum. "What brings you here?" The three took seats in big leather chairs in front of Dr. Simon's desk.

After failing miserably at trying to convince his boss back at home of the discovery of two talking 2,000-year-old squirrels, Dr. Gomez was nervous about raising the subject with another professor. He took a deep breath and began, "This is going to seem crazy . . ." He told Dr. Simon the story of Michael's discovery of Merle and Pearl, their re-animation in Tennessee, and the pursuit and eventual squirrelnapping by the man in the suit and sunglasses. To Dr. Gomez's surprise, Dr. Simon just listened and nodded, not seeming fazed in the least.

"Excuse me, Dr. Simon, may I get on your Wi-Fi?" Michael asked during a pause.

"Sure. The password's JAM3000BC. All caps," Dr. Simon responded, then said to Dr. Gomez, "It seems to me that the person most likely to be after your squirrels is Khalil Whaba."

"Khalil Whaba?" Dr. Gomez repeated. "I don't think I've ever heard of him."

"I wouldn't think you would've. He likes to lay low. Operates out of Cairo. A wealthy businessman who collects all types of ancient treasures. Things that belong in a museum like mine." Dr. Simon picked up a pen and pad of paper from the coffee table and wrote out an address. "It's about a 9-hour drive. I suggest you leave right away."

Michael looked up from his phone, which had just successfully connected to the network. "We're going to Egypt?"

"It's lovely this time of year." Dr. Simon smiled and handed Dr. Gomez the address, then stood up to see them out. Dr. Gomez thanked his old friend. Just as they were exiting the office,

Michael heard the familiar ding of a message download. As they reached the lobby of the museum, Michael pressed play on Sadie's link.

"Dad!" Michael exclaimed as they exited the museum. "It's Pearl! Where's Haifa?" He showed his dad the clip of Pearl dancing.

"It's about two hours in the opposite direction of where we were headed," Dr. Gomez replied. "But that makes much more sense. When I heard the man in the suit and sunglasses talking on the phone in the hotel back home, he was speaking Hebrew, not Arabic. It wasn't making sense to me that he'd be working for an Egyptian."

Dr. Gomez and Michael jumped in the car and headed north toward Haifa.

# CHAPTER 13

The squirrels' tiny claws clicked softly on the tiled floor of the basilica's long hallway. "Where to now?" Pearl whispered, her voice echoing off the walls.

"We need to find a way to let Michael know where we are," Merle answered. "But how?"

Suddenly, the sounds of an approaching crowd filled the hallway. Merle and Pearl scurried into a nearby alcove to avoid being seen. As the footfalls grew louder, the voice of a young woman rang out: "This church was built directly on the site believed to be the house of Mary. It was here where the angel Gabriel appeared to her and

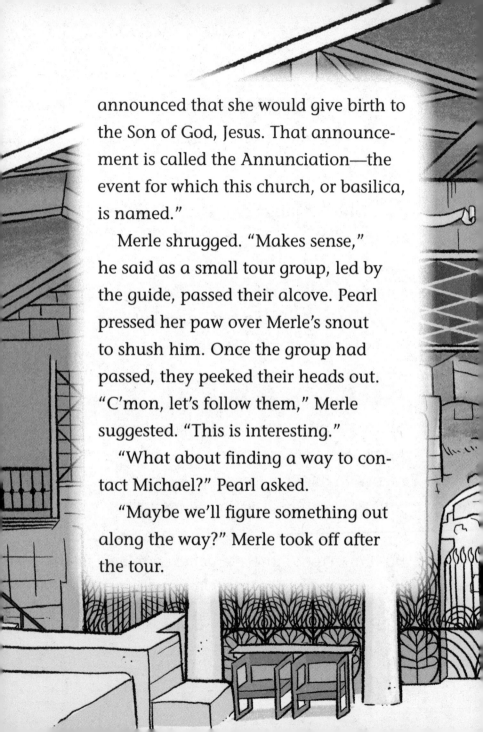

announced that she would give birth to the Son of God, Jesus. That announcement is called the Annunciation—the event for which this church, or basilica, is named."

Merle shrugged. "Makes sense," he said as a small tour group, led by the guide, passed their alcove. Pearl pressed her paw over Merle's snout to shush him. Once the group had passed, they peeked their heads out. "C'mon, let's follow them," Merle suggested. "This is interesting."

"What about finding a way to contact Michael?" Pearl asked.

"Maybe we'll figure something out along the way?" Merle took off after the tour.

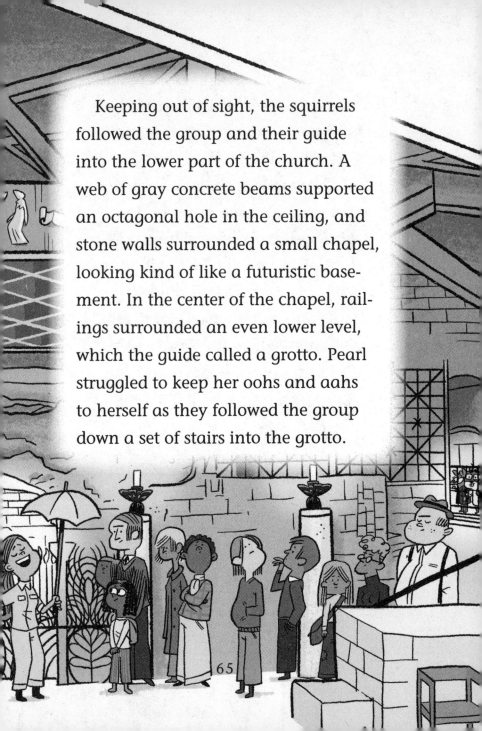

Keeping out of sight, the squirrels followed the group and their guide into the lower part of the church. A web of gray concrete beams supported an octagonal hole in the ceiling, and stone walls surrounded a small chapel, looking kind of like a futuristic basement. In the center of the chapel, railings surrounded an even lower level, which the guide called a grotto. Pearl struggled to keep her oohs and aahs to herself as they followed the group down a set of stairs into the grotto.

65

"We are now entering the Grotto of the Annunciation," the tour guide announced. "The modern church above us was built in the 1960s, but what you see here are the remains of the earliest churches on this site, dating back to the fourth century." Merle and Pearl hid behind a pillar as the guide continued, "This is the site of Mary's childhood home—where the Word was made flesh."

Since Merle and Pearl were living
in the area during the time of Jesus,
it was easy for them to imagine the
scene the tour guide described.

*When Mary was a young woman,
God sent the angel Gabriel here to
Nazareth to deliver a message to her.
Mary was engaged to be married to
a man named Joseph, a descendant
of King David.*

*"Greetings, favored woman!"
Gabriel announced. "The Lord is
with you!"*

*Mary was confused and frightened.
She tried to think of what the angel*

could mean. "The Lord is with me?"
she wondered.

"Don't be frightened," the angel
told her. "God is very happy with you.
You will become pregnant and give

birth to a son, and you will name him
Jesus. He will be very great and will be
called the Son of the Most High. The
Lord will give him the throne of his
ancestor David. And he will reign over
Israel forever; his Kingdom will never
end."

"How can this happen?" Mary
asked.

The angel replied, "The Holy
Spirit will come upon you, and the
power of the Most High will cover
you. So your baby boy will be holy,
and he will be called the Son of
God!"

Mary responded, "I am the Lord's
servant. May everything you have
said about me come true." And then
the angel left her.

"The Bible tells us, 'In the beginning the Word already existed,'" the guide explained. "'The Word was with God, and the Word was God.' Here, in this very spot, the Word became human. God became man. Jesus became a baby."

"The Word is another name for Jesus?" Merle asked in a whisper.

Pearl nodded, her eyes welling up.

# CHAPTER 15

"That's so beautiful, Merle." Pearl sniffed, ducking back behind the pillar.

"Mary was very young. That must have been scary for her," Merle whispered.

Pearl nodded. "But she trusted God and knew that he had a plan for her. That he had a plan for the whole world. He gave her the courage she needed."

"Hey!" Merle recalled, "Like Paul wrote later—when you trust God and give him your worries, he'll give you his peace."

"A good thing for all of us to remember," Pearl concluded.

Merle tapped her on the shoulder and pointed to a man in a brown robe with a rope belt walking through the chapel above the grotto. "Do you suppose he might be able to help us call Michael?" Merle asked. "He looks official." Pearl nodded in agreement, and the squirrels scurried up the stairs after the man.

In fact, the brown-robed man was a friar who served in the church. A friar is like a pastor who has taken a vow of poverty and serves people. The squirrels tracked him down a hallway and up another set of stairs into the main sanctuary of the church. Unlike the darker lower level, bright natural light flooded into the ornate cathedral through windows set into a large dome above the altar. This time,

Pearl could not keep her reactions to herself.

"Oooooh!" Pearl gasped, her tiny voice echoing off the walls. The friar turned to look but did not see the squirrels, who stood below the level of the pews. The friar then headed into one of several small wardrobe-like booths lining one of the walls of the sanctuary and closed the door. Merle pointed out an adjacent open door. "This way!"

The squirrels scurried into the booth.

"Hello?" a voice said in the darkness.

Merle jumped, startled. "Who's there?!"

"Father Phillip," the friendly

voice said with a chuckle through a darkened screen in the wall. "You were expecting someone else?"

The squirrels could now see the silhouette of the friar's head through the screen.

"We were hoping you could help us contact our friends," Pearl said.

"Hold on. I hear two different voices," Father Phillip said. "Are there two of you in there?"

"We're not very big," Merle responded.

Father Phillip laughed. "Nevertheless, this is a confessional. There's only supposed to be one of you in here at a time."

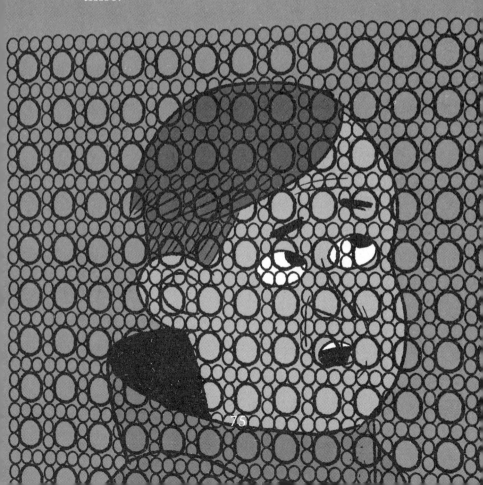

Merle and Pearl proceeded to inform the friar of their dilemma—how they had escaped their captor and were trying to get in touch with friends so that they could go home. Oh, and that they were squirrels. This last bit of information was met by silence on the other side of the screen, followed by the sound of a door opening. Suddenly, light filled Merle and Pearl's side of the confessional as a wide-eyed Father Phillip looked down. He gasped.

"You really are squirrels."

Merle and Pearl nodded in unison.

"Follow me," Father Phillip said.

# CHAPTER 16

"The dancing squirrel! I love that squirrel! She's got the moves, no?!" beamed a baggage handler, mimicking Pearl's dance as Michael held up the video on his phone.

"Yes, but did you see her come through this airport? Or any other squirrels?" Michael pleaded.

"I wish!" the handler answered, continuing to dance.

"Have you seen this squirrel?" Dr. Gomez asked a ticket agent.

"Who hasn't? I'm not a fan of rodents, but this one's adorable!" replied the agent.

"Did you see her come through the airport?" Dr. Gomez asked. The agent shook her head and shrugged.

It seemed like everyone in Haifa Airport had seen the squirrel video, but not the actual squirrels.

Michael tossed his phone into his backpack, frustrated. "What do we do, Dad?!"

"We keep looking," Dr. Gomez replied.

# CHAPTER 17

"You really are squirrels," Father Phillip repeated, still in shock.

"Yes. We've established that," Merle replied.

"Sorry. It's just . . . very new to me. How . . . when . . . what . . ." the friar stammered.

"I know it's very unusual," Pearl reassured him. She and Merle filled the friar in on their story, their relationship with Michael and Dr. Gomez, and how they desperately needed to find them.

"Yes, of course," the friar said, seeming somewhat recovered. "Do you have a phone number or email address?" He pulled his computer keyboard toward him.

Merle and Pearl looked at each other and shrugged. They were just starting to get used to the modern world and were not acquainted with the specifics of technology.

"How am I supposed to get ahold of your friends?" Father Phillip wondered.

"Well, I tried a dance

for a couple of girls on an airplane,"
Pearl said, repeating her moves.

"That's you?!" Father Phillip laughed.
"Of course! You flew into Haifa Airport.
You're the famous dancing squirrel!"

"Well, thank you," Pearl replied.
"I've always loved dancing."

"You're the what?" Merle interrupted. Since he'd been in the bathroom during Pearl's performance, he
was completely unaware of her new-
found viral fame.

"Your friends are probably headed
to Haifa. If they saw the video,

I'm sure that's where they would go," the friar deduced.

The squirrels nodded.

"I have an idea," Father Phillip continued, snapping a picture of Merle and Pearl with his phone. "I'll send two messages—one to the chaplain at the airport, an old friend. Perhaps he can be on the lookout for your friends. And one to the Antiquities Museum in Jerusalem. The director there may know how to get ahold of Dr. Gomez."

# CHAPTER 18

After searching with no luck for hours all over the airport—ticket counters, parking lots, security gates and baggage claim—Dr. Gomez and Michael found themselves at the rental car counter.

"No. Haven't seen them. I'm sorry, sir," the agent said. In fact, even though this was the very same agent who had rented a car to Ruben, he was telling the truth. Merle and

Pearl had been locked away in Ruben's luggage and out of sight of the agent.

Michael let out a frustrated sigh. "Somebody must have seen them."

"Excuse me? Dr. Gomez, Michael?" A voice suddenly rang out behind them. Michael and Dr. Gomez turned to see a man in a clerical collar walking up to them. "I understand you are looking for these two?" The airport's

chaplain held up a photo of Merle and Pearl sitting on a desk.

Michael gasped. "Where are they?!"

"They're safe and sound at the Basilica of the Annunciation in Nazareth," the chaplain replied, handing Michael the printout.

"Where's Nazareth?" Michael asked.

"About an hour to the east!" Dr. Gomez replied. They thanked the chaplain and ran toward the car.

Meanwhile . . . about two hours to the south, in Jerusalem, Dr. Simon at the Antiquities Museum read an email from an unknown friar in Nazareth. He immediately picked up his phone and made a call . . .

# CHAPTER 19

As you can imagine, Father Phillip had tons of questions for the squirrels. "I've spent my life studying the Bible, but you've lived it!" he marveled.

"Not the whole Bible," Merle pointed out. "Just the last part. We're not *that* old."

"Well, the whole Bible is about 3,500 years old, and the last part was written 2,000 years ago. So that's a pretty good chunk," Father Phillip quipped.

Pearl elbowed her husband in the ribs. "Face it, Merle. We're old." Merle waved off the comment. He didn't feel old and preferred to keep it that way.

"So, tell me more about the loaves

and fishes." Father Phillip leaned forward in his chair.

"Well," Pearl began. "It was a lovely day . . ."

# KNOCK, KNOCK, KNOCK!

Pearl's story was interrupted by someone at the door.

"That was quick!" Merle smiled. "The airport must be closer than I thought."

"A little too quick." Father Phillip glanced at his watch, concerned. The airport was at least 60 minutes away, and it had been less than an hour since he'd sent the email. "Who's there?" he called out.

How high do you suppose the chances were that the airport chaplain found Dr. Gomez and Michael immediately after reading the email Father Phillip sent? And that the Gomezes hopped in a car, sped down Highway 79 into a crowded Nazareth, found the basilica, a parking spot, and Father Phillip's office all inside of an hour?

NOT. VERY. HIGH.

The door BURST open, revealing a disheveled Ruben wearing

a sinister grin! "There you are!" Ruben grunted and dove into the room.

A flurry of scattering fur followed as Merle and Pearl ran around the small office to avoid capture. "AHHHHH! RUBEN!" Merle and Pearl shouted in unison.

"Sanctuary!" Father Phillip shouted.

"This isn't Notre-Dame, and you aren't Quasimodo!" Ruben yelled, kicking the door closed with his heel and diving after Merle, who scrambled on top of a bookcase.

"Ahhh! What does that even mean?!" Merle hollered as he zigged and zagged around Ruben's grasping hands.

The thing about most friars is that they love to teach, and some can't pass up any teachable moment, even

in a crisis. Father Phillip was one of
those. "He's referring to the book
*The Hunchback of Notre Dame* by the
nineteenth-century author Victor Hugo,
where the hunchback Quasimodo
claims 'sanctuary,' or safe haven,
for the Roma girl Esmeralda inside
the Notre-Dame cathedral," he
pontificated.

"That's nice!" Merle shouted as he jumped off the bookcase and onto the door handle, the weight of his body releasing the latch.

"I actually have that book around here somewhere . . ." the friar recalled, scanning his shelves.

Ruben rushed past him as the office door swung open and Merle and Pearl escaped into the hallway.

"Oh yes! Here it is." The friar pulled the book down and turned around to an empty room. "Hello?" he muttered.

Merle and Pearl headed for the exit, through the sanctuary and down the stairs to the main floor, Ruben following close behind.

"I'll get you!" he huffed.

"Where are we going?" Pearl shouted.

"Outside!" Merle called back, hoping to find the open window where they'd first entered the church. However, when they reached the hallway, Merle saw that the window was closed! "Uh-oh," he muttered and continued on toward the lower-level chapel.

Instinctively, squirrels head to the safety of treetops when running from trouble. However, when enclosed, like in the Dead Sea caves long ago, Merle had a way of getting himself cornered.

"Why do we keep going down?!" Pearl worried.

"I dunno?!" Merle answered, desperately. "It's the only way away from Ruben!"

With Ruben hot on their tails, they dashed through the lower-level chapel and down more stairs, only to finally hit a dead end in the ancient grotto.

"Haha!" Ruben laughed menacingly as he inched toward the squirrels, their furry backs to the wall.

"We need to work on your sense of direction," Pearl commented dryly.

"Yeah . . ." Merle replied with a gulp.

# CHAPTER 20

As the sun set behind the rolling hills
of Nazareth, Michael and Dr. Gomez
burst through the front entrance of the
basilica.

"Merle! Pearl!" Michael shouted,
his voice echoing off the walls of the
empty church.

"They've gone," a somber voice rang
out from the shadows. Father Phillip
stepped out into a pool of cool moon-
light near the railing surrounding the
Grotto of the Annunciation. "A man
came and took them."

"He was wearing a suit and sunglasses," Michael guessed.

"As a matter of fact, he was," Father

Phillip said. "The squirrels called him
Ruben."

"Ruben . . ." Dr. Gomez noted. It was
the first time Michael and Dr. Gomez
had heard the name of the mysterious
figure.

Michael's eyes welled up. Feeling
overwhelmed, hungry, and tired from
jet lag, he couldn't help but cry.

Besides teaching, another thing friars do well is to comfort those who are troubled. "I know you are afraid for your friends," Father Phillip said as he put his hand on Michael's shoulder. "Remember Mary, who was very young when Gabriel came to visit her at this very spot. She, too, was afraid of an uncertain future. What would it be like being the mother of Jesus? But the angel assured her that nothing is impossible with God. That is true for you as well. Whenever you are worried or scared, you can pray for God's peace."

"My dad tells me the same thing," Michael said, exchanging a grin with Dr. Gomez. "Can we pray now?"

"This is a good place for that," Father Phillip said with a smile.

There in the quiet church, Michael prayed again for help finding Merle and Pearl. He asked God to help him not feel afraid or worried. "And God, we know that you are in control and nothing is impossible with you. In Jesus' name, amen."

"Well, buddy, it's late," Dr. Gomez said. "We'd better find a room in an inn somewhere around here." Dr. Gomez thanked Father Phillip for his help and for getting the word to him about Merle and Pearl. "By the way," Dr. Gomez asked, "how do you think Ruben found you?"

"The only thing that makes sense to me is that I also sent an email to the Antiquities Museum in Jerusalem. Maybe that's how Ruben got the information?" Father Phillip speculated.

Dr. Gomez shook his head in disbelief.

Michael's jaw dropped.

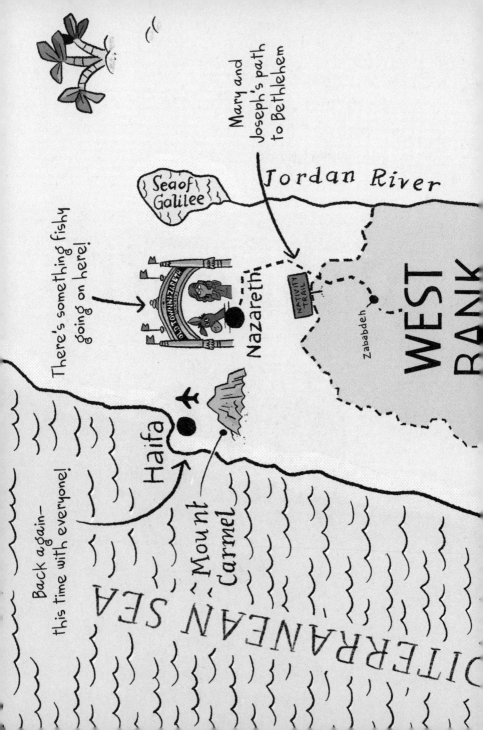

Tel Aviv
Dr. Simon's nefarious plans!
SAFE HOUSE
DONKEY HAVEN
Animal Sanctuary
Dusty makes a break for it!
Ein Karem
Jerusalem
Bethlehem
Dead Sea
There's no place Merle would rather NOT be!
I can't feel my legs!

**MICHAEL GOMEZ** is an adventurous and active 10-year-old boy. He is kindhearted but often acts before he thinks. He's friendly and talkative and blissfully unaware that most of his classmates think he's a bit geeky. Michael is super excited to be in fifth grade, which, in his mind, makes him "grade school royalty!"

**MERLE SQUIRREL** may be thousands of years old, but he never really grew up. He has endless enthusiasm for anything new and interesting—especially this strange modern world he finds himself in. He marvels at the self-refilling bowl of fresh drinking water (otherwise known as a toilet) and supplements his regular diet of tree nuts with what he believes might be the world's most perfect food: chicken nuggets. He's old enough to know better, but he often finds it hard to do better. Good thing he's got his wife, Pearl, to help him make wise choices.

**PEARL SQUIRREL** is wise beyond her many, many, many years, with enough common sense for both her and Merle. When Michael's in a bind, she loves to share a lesson or bit of wisdom from Bible events she witnessed in her youth. Pearl's biggest quirk is that she is a nut hoarder. Having come from a world where food is scarce, her instinct is to grab whatever she can. The abundance and variety of nuts in present-day Tennessee can lead to distraction and storage issues.

**JUSTIN KESSLER** is Michael's best friend. Justin is quieter and has better judgment than Michael, and he is super smart. He's a rule follower and is obsessed with being on time. He'll usually give in to what Michael wants to do after warning him of the likely consequences.

**SADIE HENDERSON** is Michael and Justin's other best friend. She enjoys video games and bowling just as much as cheerleading and pajama parties. She gets mad respect from her classmates as the only kid at Walnut Creek Elementary who's not afraid of school bully Edgar. Though Sadie's in a different homeroom than her two best friends, the three always sit together at lunch and hang out after class.

**DR. GOMEZ,** a professor of anthropology, is not thrilled when he finds out that his son, Michael, smuggled two ancient squirrels home from their summer trip to the Dead Sea, but he ends up seeing great value in having them around as original sources for his research. Dad loves his son's adventurous spirit but wishes Michael would look (or at least peek) before he leaps.

**MRS. GOMEZ** teaches part-time at her daughter's preschool and is a full-time mom to Michael and Jane. She feels sorry for the fish-out-of-water squirrels and looks for ways to help them feel at home, including constructing and decorating an over-the-top hamster mansion for Merle and Pearl in Michael's room. She also can't help but call Michael by her favorite (and his least favorite) nickname, Cookies.

**MR. NEMESIS** is the Gomez family cat who becomes Merle and Pearl's true nemesis. Jealous of the time and attention given to the squirrels by his family, Mr. Nemesis is continuously coming up with brilliant and creative ways to get rid of them. He hides his ability to talk from the family, but not the squirrels.

**JANE GOMEZ** is Michael's little sister. She's super adorable but delights in getting her brother busted so she can be known as the "good child." She thinks Merle and Pearl are the cutest things she has ever seen in her whole life (next to Mr. Nemesis) and is fond of dressing them up in her doll clothes.

**RUBEN,** previously known only as "the man in the suit and sunglasses," has been on the squirrels' tails ever since Michael discovered them at the Dead Sea. Ruben is determined to capture and deliver the refugee rodents to his boss in Israel. He's clever and inventive, but then again, so are the squirrels! Ruben struggles to stay one step ahead of Merle and Pearl.

**DR. SIMON** is the director of the Jerusalem Antiquities Museum and Ruben's boss. The mastermind behind the creation of the world's first and largest talking-animal petting zoo, he'll stop at nothing to make sure Merle and Pearl headline the grand opening of his theme park alongside a bevy of other babbling biblical beasts.

**FATHER PHILLIP** is a kind and helpful friar who first encounters Merle and Pearl at the Basilica of the Annunciation in Nazareth. He becomes a trusted local ally of Dr. Gomez and Michael, keeping an ear to the ground for the whereabouts of the squirrels as they are smuggled about Israel.

**ADRIANA** hails from South America (like all alpacas), so how did she end up in Israel? No one knows for sure, but what is certain is that Adriana is the best friend a donkey could ask for and president of the Dusty Fan Club. She can't speak, but she can pick locks with her lips and has a knack for being in the right place at the right time.

**DUSTY** is a retired Holy Land tour donkey, purchased by Ruben for agorot on the shekel (pennies on the dollar) to transport Merle and Pearl from Galilee to Judea. The squirrels soon discover that Dusty can also speak human and is a direct descendant of Balaam's donkey of biblical fame.

# DR. GOMEZ'S
## Historical Handbook

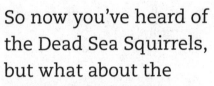

So now you've heard of the Dead Sea Squirrels, but what about the **DEAD SEA *SCROLLS*?**

Way back in 1946, just after the end of World War II, in a cave along the banks of the Dead Sea, a 15-year-old boy came across some jars containing ancient scrolls while looking after his goats. When scholars and archaeologists found out about his discovery, the hunt for more scrolls was on! Over the next 10 years, many more scrolls and pieces of scrolls were found in 11 different caves.

117

There are different theories about exactly who wrote on the scrolls and hid them in the caves. One of the most popular ideas is that they belonged to a group of Jewish priests called Essenes, who lived in the desert because they had been thrown out of Jerusalem. One thing is for sure—the scrolls are very, very old! They were placed in the caves between the years 300 BC and AD 100!

Forty percent of the words on the scrolls come from the Bible. Parts of every Old Testament book except for the book of Esther have been discovered.

Of the remaining 60 percent, half are religious texts not found in the Bible, and half are historical records about the way people lived 2,000 years ago.

The discovery of the Dead Sea Scrolls is one of the most important archaeological finds in history!

# About the Author

As co-creator of VeggieTales, co-founder of Big Idea Entertainment, and the voice of the beloved Larry the Cucumber, **MIKE NAWROCKI** has been dedicated to helping parents pass on biblical values to their kids through storytelling for over two decades. Mike currently serves as assistant professor of film and animation at Lipscomb University in Nashville, Tennessee, and makes his home in nearby Franklin with his wife, Lisa, and their two children. The Dead Sea Squirrels is Mike's first children's book series.

Find out what happens next in
*A Dusty Donkey Detour!*

# SADDLE UP AND JOIN WINNIE AND HER FAMILY AT THE WILLIS WYOMING RANCH!

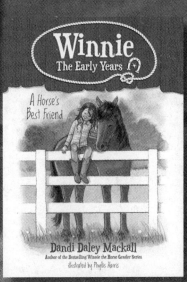

Winnie is the star of the bestselling Winnie the Horse Gentler series that sold more than half a million copies and taught kids around the world about faith, kindness, and horse training. Winnie could ride horses before she could walk, but training them is another story. In this new series, eight-year-old Winnie learns the fine art of horse gentling from her horse wrangler mom as they work together to save the family ranch.

Join twelve-year-old Winnie Willis and her friends—
both human and animal—on their adventures through
paddock and pasture as they learn about caring for
others, trusting God, and growing up.

Collect all eight Winnie the Horse Gentler books.
Or get the complete collection with the Barn Boxed Set!